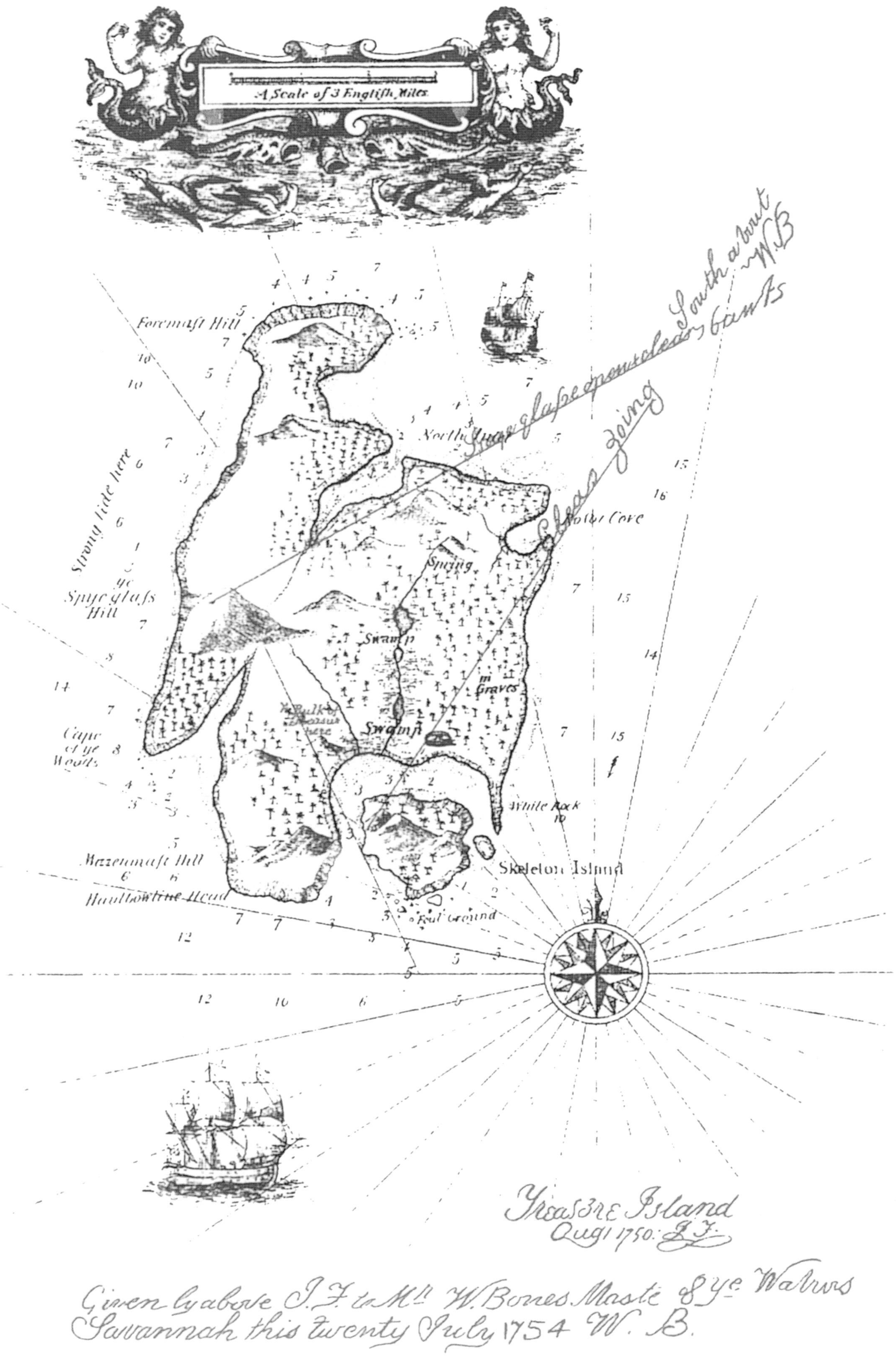

A Scale of 3 English Miles.

Foremast Hill

Strong tide here

ye Spye glass Hill

Cape of ye Woods

Mizzenmast Hill

Haullowtrue Head

North Inlet

Spring

Swamp

ye Bulk of Treasure here

Swamp

Graves

Swamp

Spye glass

South about

Sea open to clear banks

Glass going

Noise Cove

White Rock

Skeleton Island

Foul Ground

Treasure Island
Augt 1750. J.F.

Given by above J.F. to Mr. W. Bones Maste of ye Walrus
Savannah this twenty July 1754 W. B.

Facsimile of Chart: latitude and
longitude struck out by J Hawkins

W.B

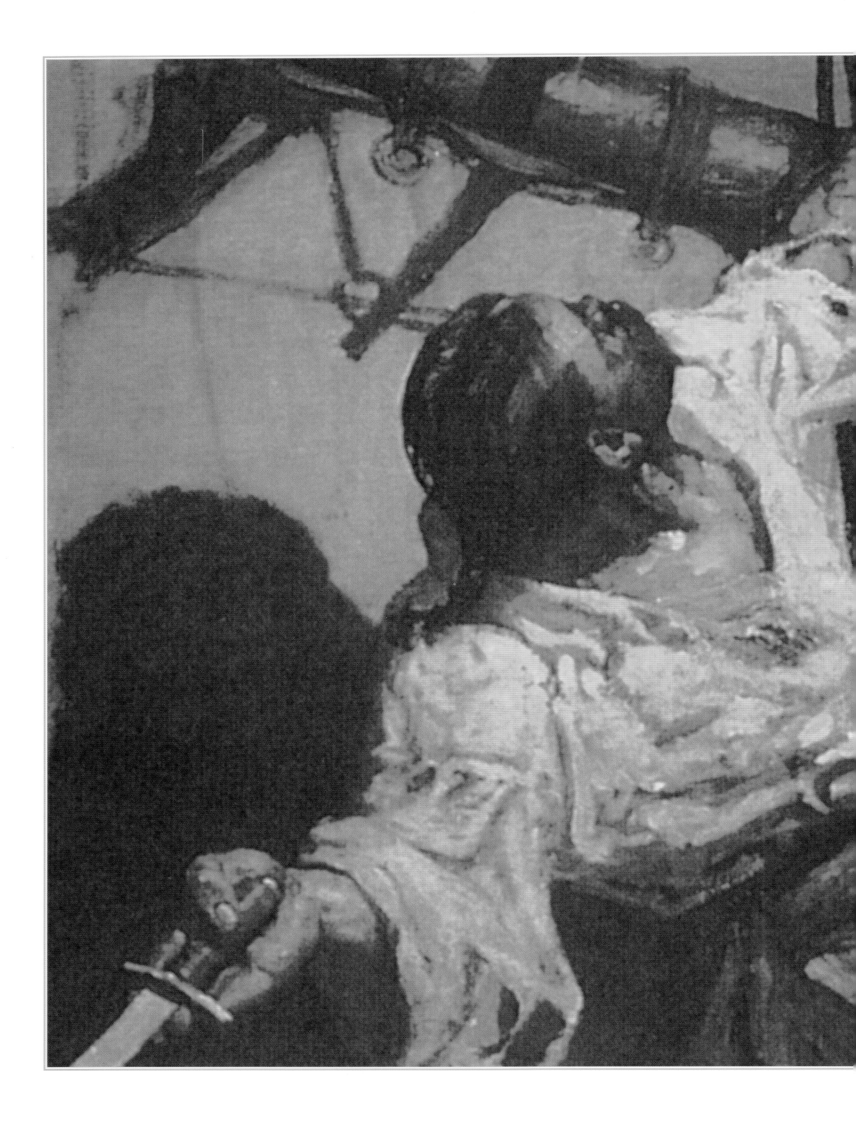

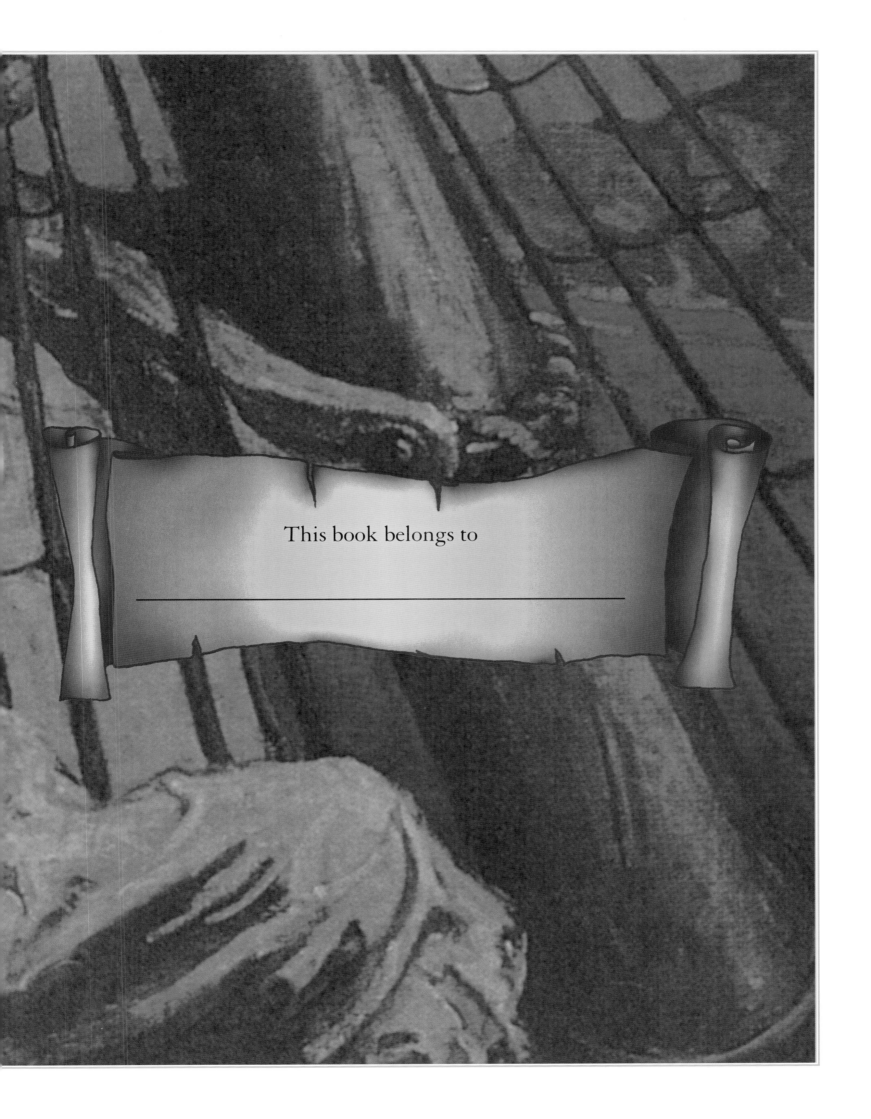

This book belongs to

_____

9   8   7   6   5   4   3   2   1
Digit on the right indicates the number of this printing

Library of Congress Cataloging-in-Publication Number 2001094075

ISBN 0-7624-1275-5

Cover design by Melissa Allard
Interior design by Ellen Lohse
Retold by Steven Zorn
Edited by Susan K. Hom
Typography: Granjon and French Script

This book may be ordered by mail from the publisher.
But try your bookstore first!

Published by Courage Books, an imprint of
Running Press Book Publishers
125 South Twenty-second Street
Philadelphia, Pennsylvania 19103-4399

Visit us on the web!
www.runningpress.com

TREASURE ISLAND

A Young Reader's Edition of the Classic Adventure

by Robert Louis Stevenson
Illustrated by N.C. Wyeth

COURAGE
BOOKS

AN IMPRINT OF RUNNING PRESS
PHILADELPHIA • LONDON

Squire Trelawney, Dr. Livesey and the rest of these gentlemen have asked me to write down everything that happened on Treasure Island. The story starts at my home, the Admiral Benbow Inn. That was the name of the inn that my father ran, and that's where I first saw the old seaman. He came in dragging his sea-chest behind him. He was a tall, strong, heavy, nut-brown man with a pigtail that fell over the shoulders of his soiled blue coat. His hands were ragged and scarred, with black, broken nails. A scar ran across one cheek. He looked around the room, whistling to himself. Then he broke out into that old sea-song that he'd sing so often afterwards:

"Fifteen men on the dead man's chest—
Yo-ho-ho, and a bottle of rum!"

After looking around, he decided to stay. "You can call me captain," he said as he tossed down some gold pieces to pay for his room and board. He seemed like a man accustomed to be obeyed or to strike.

He was a very silent man by custom. All day he hung round the cove, or upon the cliffs, with a brass telescope; all evening he sat in a corner of the parlor next to the fire, and drank rum and water. Mostly he would not speak when spoken to. He'd look up sudden and fierce, and blow through his nose like a foghorn. We and the people who came to our house soon learned to let him be.

Every day when he came back from his stroll, he would ask if any seafaring men had gone by along the road. We could tell he wanted to avoid them. He took me aside one day and promised me a silver fourpenny on the first day of every month if I would keep a lookout for a sailor with one leg. I was to let him know the moment he appeared.

I was terrified by the idea of the sailor with one leg. I was far less afraid of the captain, who managed to frighten everyone else at the Admiral Benbow Inn. He would tell dreadful stories about hanging, and walking the plank, and storms at sea. Then he would sing "Yo-ho-ho, and a bottle of rum," and make the neighbors join in. He wouldn't allow anyone to leave until he was

All day he hung round the cove, or upon the cliffs, with a brass telescope . . .

Just at the door, the captain aimed at Black Dog one last tremendous cut . . .

done. Everyone was afraid of him. My father feared he was driving away business. What's worse, the captain stayed week after week, month after month. My father was too afraid of him to ask him for more money for his room.

By winter, my father had taken ill, and was unlikely to see the spring. Our unpleasant captain was still with us. On a bitter January morning, he left the house early and set out to the beach. His cutlass was swinging under the broad skirts of his old blue coat, his brass telescope was tucked under his arm. My mother went upstairs to tend to my father. I was putting out the breakfast dishes when a stranger walked into the parlor. He was a pale creature, missing two fingers on his left hand. Though he wore a cutlass, he did not look much like a fighter. I had always had my eye open for seafaring men, with one leg or two. This man wasn't a sailor, but he had something of the sea about him. He asked if his mate Bill was staying here; he described the captain. I told him his mate was out walking and when he might expect him to return.

The stranger kept hanging around just inside the inn door, peering around the corner like a cat waiting for a mouse. I didn't know what to do, but I decided it was none of my business.

Soon the stranger spied the captain returning to the house. "We'll give Bill a little surprise," he said. He put me behind him in the corner of the parlor, both hidden by the open door. I was uneasy and alarmed, and so, it seemed was the stranger. He loosened the cutlass in its sheath.

At last in strode the captain, slammed the door behind him, and marched to the breakfast table.

"Bill," said the stranger, in a voice that I thought he had tried to make bold and big.

The captain spun around. "Black Dog!" said he, as all the color drained out of his face. They asked for rum. I brought it, then left the room.

All of a sudden there was a tremendous explosion of noises—a chair and table went over in a lump, a clash of steel followed, and then a cry of pain. Black Dog went running toward the door. The captain followed close behind, waving his cutlass. Just at the door, the captain aimed at Black Dog one last tremendous cut, which would certainly have split him had it not been stopped by our big signboard of Admiral Benbow Inn. You can still see the notch.

Black Dog was on the road and over the hill in half a minute. The captain, unsteady, asked for more rum, and then collapsed on the floor.

Doctor Livesey, who had come to check on my poor, sick father, rushed to help the captain. He gave us medicine for him, put him to bed, and told us to keep him there at least a week. When the captain finally awakened, he was not pleased with the news.

"Thunder!" he cried. "A week! I can't do that; they'd have the black spot on me by then." He tried to rise from the bed, but didn't have the strength.

"What's the black spot?" I asked.

"It's not good, Jim," he replied. He rested for a while, and then said to me, "That man who was here today—Black Dog—he's a bad one. But there's worse. If they come here, they're after my sea-chest. There's something in there they want. It was given to me by Captain Flint, the pirate, before he died. I sailed with him. So did Black Dog, and the man with one leg. Don't let these men get what's in my chest." I gave him his medicine and before long he fell asleep.

The days passed. The captain managed to get out of bed, but he was still very weak. During that time, my father died, and I had little time to think about the captain.

The day after the funeral, while I was still full of sad thoughts about my father, I saw a blind beggar coming down the road, tapping his stick ahead of himself. He wore a tattered old cloak with a hood. He was hunched over from age or weakness. As he drew nearer to the inn, he asked aloud for someone to tell him where he was.

"You are at the Admiral Benbow Inn," I told him. I held out my hand and in an instant he gripped it like a vice.

"Take me to the captain, then," he snarled, "or I'll break your arm." He grasped tighter. I cried out in pain. I took him to see the captain. I had no choice.

The captain was seated in the parlor. When he saw the blind man, his face went pale. He tried to rise but was too weak. The blind man ordered him to put out his left palm. The captain did as he was told, and the blind man passed something into it. Whatever it was, the captain closed his hand around it without looking at it. Then the blind man released his grip on me, nimbly left the inn and scurried down the road.

The captain slowly opened his palm and saw what was inside. He sprang to his feet, and in the same instant put his hand to his throat and collapsed onto the floor, dead.

I told my mother all that the captain had said to me about the sea-chest. We knew we could no longer stay at the inn for fear that the blind beggar—or worse— would return. We left the captain's body on the floor and rode our horses to the next village to get help. But nobody would help us, for fear of the pirates who had once worked for Captain Flint.

One of the townspeople rode off to summon Dr. Livesey for us. Another gave me a loaded pistol. That was all they would offer. My mother and I rode home, alone in the dark, to face whatever waited for us back at the inn.

We got there, and I bolted the door at once. We stood and panted for a moment in the dark, alone in the house with the dead captain's body. My mother lit a candle. I drew the blinds. Now we had to look for the key to the sea-chest. We supposed the captain had it in his pocket.

I went down on my knees at once. On the floor close to his hand there was a little round of paper, blackened on one side. I could not doubt that this was the black spot. I picked it up. On the other side was written: "You have till ten tonight."

Just as I read it, the clock struck, startling me shockingly. But the news was good, for it was only six.

I searched the captain's pockets but found no key.

"Perhaps it's round his neck," suggested my mother.

With great reluctance, I tore open his shirt at the neck. There hung the key.

We ran upstairs to the captain's room and opened the chest. The inside smelled of tobacco and tar. Mostly the chest was filled with souvenirs of his travels, along with compasses, a suit of clothes, and some pistols. Then underneath all this lay a bundle of papers and a canvas bag of gold coins from many different countries.

Mother began counting out the money that the captain owed us for his stay at the inn. Halfway through, I suddenly put my hand upon her arm; for I had heard in the silent, frosty air, the horrible tap-tapping of the blind man's stick upon the frozen road. It drew nearer. We held our breath. Then it struck sharp on the inn door. We could hear the handle being turned, and the bolt rattling as the blind man tried to enter. Then a few moments of silence. At last the tapping started again, mercifully fading away as the unwelcome visitor left us.

"Mother," said I, "let's be going. He's sure to return with others."

As we left the inn, the moon was high and bright. We weren't far when we heard the approaching sound of footsteps and shouts in the distance. Mother fainted, and I had to carry her to the side of a small, nearby bridge where we hid. But it was not a good place, and we could easily be discovered.

I was able to still see the inn. Seven or eight men arrived. One of them was the blind beggar. He ordered the others to break down the door. Some of the men rushed inside. I heard the bangs and crashes as the contents of the captain's chest was spilled out and searched.

"Pew," cried one of the men in the house, "It's gone."

The blind man, Pew, told them to check the captain's pockets.

"Bill's been overhauled already," replied another voice from inside the house, "there's nothing left."

"It's that boy!" shouted blind Pew. "Spread out and find him."

The men started arguing that the captain's doubloons were still in the chest, and they'd be happy to split them. But Pew wouldn't settle. He wanted something else that was in that chest. Something worth much more.

As the men argued and fought, the sound of galloping horses closed in. The men scattered in every direction, leaving Pew behind. He went tapping up and down the road in a frenzy, groping and calling for his comrades. He ran a few steps past me, crying:

"Johnny, Black Dog, Dirk," and other names, "you won't leave old Pew, mates—not old Pew!"

The sound of the galloping horses grew nearer. Pew made a dash and screamed as he stumbled into a ditch. He was on his feet again in a second and made another dash, right

He went tapping up and down the road in a frenzy, groping and calling for his comrades.

I said goodbye to mother and the cove where I had lived since I was born, and to the Old Admiral Benbow Inn.

under the nearest of the speeding horses. The rider tried to save him, but it was too late. Pew was dead.

By now the other riders had approached. They were officers fetched by the man in the village. They took my mother and me to the village, where my mother awakened from her fainting spell. We told the officers what had happened. Afterwards, I asked to be taken to Dr. Livesey's house. I had something important to share.

The doctor greeted me and introduced me to squire Trelawney. When we were settled, I pulled from my pocket an oilcloth packet that I had removed from the captain's chest. Dr. Livesey opened it. Inside was a record of all the ships that Flint the pirate had pillaged, along with a map that showed where he'd buried all their riches.

We knew what we had to do next: hire a ship and a crew, and go find that treasure.

The ship we bought was called the *Hispaniola* and we hired a crew of seasoned sailors. Among them was an old salt named Long John Silver, who was to be the ship's cook. He'd lost one of his legs in the war, but John Trelawney, who hired him, said he got along as well as any man with two legs.

I was to be the ship's cabin boy. Soon the ship was stocked and ready to sail. I said goodbye to mother and the cove where I had lived since I was born, and to the old Admiral Benbow Inn. One of my last thoughts was of the captain, who had so often strode along the beach with his cocked hat, his sabre-cut cheek, and his old brass telescope. Next moment we had turned the corner, and my home was out of sight.

We were still in port when our troubles began. Mr. Trelawney and the captain didn't get along. The captain's name was Smollett, and he asked to speak with Mr. Trelawney, who was to be the ship's admiral on this adventure.

Captain Smollett said to Mr. Trelawney, "Sir, I don't like this cruise. I don't trust the crew."

"Why not?" asked Mr. Trelawney.

"When I was hired, I was told that the purpose of this trip was a secret. I wasn't told where we were going or why. But now I've learned that the whole crew knows that we're after treasure. Treasure cruises are dangerous. I don't like them."

Mr. Trelawney was surprised to hear that the crew knew the purpose of the trip.

"I'll tell you what else I've heard," continued the captain. "You have a treasure map of an island, and that island lies—"
And he named the exact latitude and longitude of the place.

We all were shocked. The captain said everyone aboard knew where we were heading. Mr. Trelawney assured him he'd keep his eye on the crew. There was nothing else to do.

At dawn the next morning, we weighed anchor. Long John Silver, with his crutch under his arm, stood by to watch. As the men hoisted the chains, he broke into the song I knew so well—

"Fifteen men on the dead man's chest:—

And then the whole crew sang the chorus—

"Yo-ho-ho, and a bottle of rum!"

At the third "ho!" they pulled the chain with great force.

At last the ship pulled away from the port and out to sea we sailed. The *Hispaniola* was a good ship. Everyone aboard did his job well. Everyone seemed to get along. The whole crew respected and obeyed the ship's cook, Long John Silver. They called him "Barbecue."

"He's no common man, Barbecue," said the coxswain to me. "He had good schooling in his

To me he was very kind, and always glad to see me in the galley, which he kept clean as a new pin.

young days, and can speak like a book when he wants to. And he's brave—a lion is nothing alongside Long John!"

Long John had a way of talking to each sailor, and doing favors for them. To me he was very kind, and always glad to see me in the galley, which he kept clean as a new pin. He kept the dishes in order, and his parrot stayed in a cage in one corner.

"Come away, Hawkins," he would say, "come and have a yarn with John. Nobody more welcome than yourself, my son. Sit down and hear the news. Here's Cap'n Flint—I call my parrot Cap'n Flint, after the famous buccaneer. Here's Cap'n Flint predicting success to our voyage. Weren't you, Cap'n?" And the parrot would say, over and over, "Pieces of eight! Pieces of eight! Pieces of eight!" until you wondered why it was not out of breath. Or until John threw his handkerchief over the cage.

When I first heard that the ship's cook had but one leg, I worried. What if he was the seaman the captain had told me to keep a lookout for? But having seen bad men like blind Pew and Black Dog, I knew what bad men were like. And I was sure that Long John Silver was no buccaneer. Like everyone else, I trusted him completely.

⚬

On we sailed. Soon it was about the last day of our voyage. Sometime that night or by noon of the next day, Treasure Island would be seen. Everyone was in the best spirits because we were now so near an end to the first part of our adventure.

Just after sundown, when all my work was done, I grew hungry for an apple. I ran on deck. The apple barrel was big and deep, and had scarcely an apple in it. I had to climb in to find one. I sat down in the dark bottom of the barrel. The sound of the water and the gentle rocking of the ship began to lull me to sleep. Just then, a heavy man sat down with rather a clash close by. The barrel shook as he leaned his shoulders against it. I was just about to jump up when the man began to speak. It was Silver's voice. Before I had heard a dozen words, I knew I shouldn't speak. From these dozen words I understood that the lives of all the honest men aboard depended on me alone.

From the apple barrel, I could hear Long John Silver talking to two or three men. They were excited.

"When are we going to strike?" growled one of the men.

"When!" shouted Silver. "I'll tell you when. At the last possible moment. After the treasure's on board. Or maybe we'll wait until Captain Smollett has sailed us halfway home."

That's when I knew the truth: Long John Silver and these men were pirates. They were plotting to do away with every honest man once the treasure was safely on board. We were in great danger.

Just then a sort of brightness fell upon me in the barrel, and looking up, I found the moon had risen high and bright. Almost at that same time the voice of the lookout shouted "Land ho!"

There was a great rush of feet across the deck. I could hear people tumbling up from the cabin. Slipping in an instant out of the apple barrel, I came out on the open deck in time to join the others.

Away to the southwest we saw two low hills, about a couple of miles apart, and rising behind one of them a third and higher hill, whose peak was still buried in the fog.

"And now then," said the captain, "has any of you ever seen that land ahead?"

"I have, sir," said Silver. "Skeleton Island they calls it. It were a main place for pirates once."

"Thank you, my man," said Captain Smollett.

I wanted to tell the captain right away about the terrible danger we were in, but I had to wait until we could speak in private. Some time later, I saw my chance. Dr. Livesey, Mr. Trelawney, and Captain Smollett were seated around a table in the captain's quarters. I told them what I had heard. No one interrupted me. Then the captain spoke.

"First point," he began. "We must go on, because we can't turn back. If they think we know they're pirates, they'll attack at once. Second point, we're safe until the treasure's found. Third point, not all of them are pirates. There must be some loyal men aboard. We should find them and attack the pirates before the pirates attack us."

They determined that out of twenty-six men on board, perhaps seven of them could be trusted. But one of those six was just a boy—me.

Loaded pistols were given to all the men we believed were on our side.

When I came on deck the next morning, the look of the island had changed. The sun shone bright and hot, and the shore birds were fishing and crying all around us, but my heart sank. I hated the very thought of Treasure Island. Under the scorching sun, we brought the ship around to the narrow passage between Treasure Island and the smaller Skeleton Island.

The crew was getting restless. They were fighting with each other and also with Long John Silver. We knew that Silver was the real captain of these pirates, but he couldn't act that way in front of Captain Smollett. Smollett thought it would be a good idea to let them go ashore so that Silver could control them better. That would also give us time to make our own plans against the pirates.

Loaded pistols were given to all the men we believed were on our side. They stayed behind while most of Silver's men boarded the boats to row ashore. At the last moment, I had the wild idea to go ashore with them. I slipped over the side of the ship and hid beneath some sheets. My boat was the first to reach the shore. The second it got there, I bounded out and ran into the woods. I could hear Silver shouting, "Jim! Jim!" but I paid him no attention. I ran until I could run no longer.

Feeling safe, I began to explore this strange, new place. No person lived here, just animals and birds. Here and there were flowering plants. Here and there I saw snakes and other creatures.

I made my way to a marsh. All at once I saw a bustle among the bulrushes. A wild duck flew up with a quack, another followed, and soon the whole surface of the marsh was covered by a great cloud of birds. They hung circling and screaming in the air. They had been frightened by the approach of human visitors. Soon I heard other voices myself.

In great fear, I hid under the cover of a live oak tree, and squatted quiet as a mouse. One of the voices was Long John Silver's. The other was a crewman named Tom. They drew nearer and then stopped to talk seriously. I could tell that Silver was trying to convince Tom to join his gang of thieves. I was glad to hear Tom refusing the offer. I had found one of the honest men.

Then all of a sudden he was interrupted by the sound of a horrifying scream. The whole island echoed from it and the cloud of birds rose again.

Tom had leaped at the sound. "What was that?" he asked.

"That?" said Silver, smiling. "I reckon that would be Alan."

"Alan!" cried Tom. "You've killed Alan, have you? Rest his soul for being an honest seaman. Now more than ever I'm sure I'll not join your thieves. Kill me, too, if you can. But I defy you."

Through the leaves I could see Tom turn and walk away. He didn't get far. With a shout, Silver grabbed a tree branch for balance, pulled his crutch from under his arm and threw it like a spear. It hit Tom hard between the shoulders, knocking him to the ground. Then I saw Silver pull a knife, and, even on one leg, rush toward Tom. That was the end of an honest sailor.

Long John Silver put his hand in his pocket, pulled out a whistle, and blew a series of loud blasts. I didn't know what it meant, but I feared that more men would be coming. The buccaneers had killed two honest men. I didn't want to be next.

I began to crawl back through the woods as quietly as I could. I began to hear the men approaching. I couldn't let them find me. As soon as I was out of the woods, I ran as I never ran before. As I ran, fear grew and grew upon me. I paid no attention to where I was going, and was soon lost. I kept running, thinking I would never see the *Hispaniola*, Dr. Livesey, or Mr. Trelawney again. As I ran past the bottom of a steep hill, my fear grew because of what happened next.

From the side of the hill, some gravel suddenly came tumbling down. I looked. Through the trees, I saw a figure leap very quickly behind the trunk of a pine. Whether it was a bear, or man, or monkey, I couldn't tell. It seemed dark and shaggy. My terror brought me to a standstill with a thumping heart.

I was now, it seemed, cut off from both sides. Behind me were the murderers; before me was this lurking creature. Long John Silver himself seemed less terrible than this unknown beast. I began to retrace my steps in the direction of the boats.

Instantly the figure reappeared. It began to head me off. From trunk to trunk the creature flitted like a deer, running manlike on two legs, but unlike any man that I had ever seen. It stooped almost double as it ran. Yet, now I was sure it was a man.

Through the trees, I saw a figure leap very quickly behind the trunk of a pine.

I began to recall what I had heard about cannibals. Then I remembered I had a gun, and I felt more secure. Of course, I wouldn't attack him unless he attacked me. But now I grew curious, and went to find him.

He was hiding behind a tree trunk. He must have been watching me closely, for as soon as I began to move in his direction he came out and took a step to meet me. He paused, drew back, and came forward again. Then, to my wonder and confusion, he threw himself on his knees and held out his hands toward me.

"Who are you?" I asked.

"Ben Gunn," he answered, and his voice sounded hoarse and awkward, like a rusty lock. "I'm poor Ben Gunn, I am. I haven't spoken to anyone for three years."

His skin, wherever it was exposed behind his tattered clothes, was burned from the sun. His clothes were a patchwork of old canvas and sea cloth. They were held together by brass buttons, bits of stick and other odd fastenings.

"Three years!" I cried. "Were you shipwrecked?"

"Nay, mate," said he—"marooned."

I had heard the word and knew it stood for a horrible kind of punishment common among the buccaneers. A marooned man is put ashore on a distant, empty island with no hope of getting off.

"Marooned three years," he continued, "and lived on goats since then, and berries and oysters. I've longed for other food. Many's the long night I've dreamed of cheese—toasted, mostly—and woke up again, without it."

"If ever I can get aboard again," said I, "you shall have plenty of cheese."

"What do you call yourself, mate?" he asked.

"Jim," I told him.

"Well, now, Jim," he said, lowering his voice to a whisper. "Let me tell you something— I'm rich."

I felt sure this poor fellow had gone crazy from being alone on the island so long. He continued talking.

"Rich! Rich! I says. And I'll tell you what: I'll make you rich, too, Jim, because you were the first one that found me!"

Then a frightened look came over his face. He raised a finger in front of my eyes.

"Now, Jim, you tell me true: that ain't Flint's ship?" he asked.

"It's not Flint's ship. Flint, the pirate, is dead. But some of Flint's hands are aboard. Bad luck for the rest of us."

"Not a man—with one—leg?" he gasped.

"Silver?" I asked.

"Ah, Silver!" says he; "That were his name."

"He's the cook. And the ringleader, too." I told Ben Gunn the whole story of our adventure—and our problems.

"Well, you just put your trust in Ben Gunn—Ben Gunn's the man to do it," he said, promising to help us.

He told me how he ended up on Treasure Island.

"I were on Flint's ship when he buried the treasure," he started. "Him and six strong seamen. They all went ashore, but only Flint came back. Nobody knows how he killed them, but all six were dead. Only Flint knew where the treasure was buried.

"Three years ago," Gunn continued, "I was on another ship, and we sighted this island. 'Boys' said I, 'here's Flint's treasure. Let's land and find it.' The captain wasn't pleased, but my messmates all wanted to look for the treasure, so we landed. Twelve days they searched, and each day they grew angrier with me. Then, one fine morning, they all went aboard. 'As for you, Benjamin Gunn,' says they to me, 'here's a musket, and a spade, and a pickaxe. You can stay here and find Flint's money for yourself.'

"Well, Jim," continued Gunn, "I haven't seen a single person since then." He asked me to go back to the ship to tell Mr. Trelawney that Gunn could help us.

"How am I to get on board?" I asked.

"Well," answered Gunn, "I have a boat. I made it with my own hands. It's hidden under the white rock. If worst comes to worst, we might try that after dark."

Just then, the whole island echoed with the thunder of a cannon.

"They have begun to fight!" I cried. "Follow me."

I began to run toward the boats. The marooned man in his goatskins trotted easily close to my side. The cannon-shot was followed by the sounds of small guns. Then, a quarter of a mile in front of me, the Union Jack fluttered in the air above the woods.

The Stockade

While Jim Hawkins was ashore, Captain Smollett, Mr. Trelawney, Dr. Livesey, and another man remained on the ship, along with six of the mutineers. Dr. Livesey could see on the treasure map that nearby, on the shore, stood a small building. The doctor and another man left the ship to investigate it.

It was a sturdy log shelter, built with a tall wall, a stockade, around it to protect the men inside. Nearby, a spring provided fresh water. Holes in the walls were designed to fire rifles through to ward off attackers. The doctor decided that he and his men would be safer in this stockade than on the ship. He rowed back to the ship to tell the other honest men of his plan.

Armed with pistols, the men forced the mutineers below deck where they couldn't warn Long John Silver or the rest of the pirates who were ashore. The doctor then loaded a small boat with supplies: pork, powder, biscuits, and five guns and cutlasses. He dropped the rest of the weapons into the sea where they could do no harm.

The men had made four easy trips from the ship to the stockade. The fifth trip was much harder. Their small rowboat was overloaded. The current changed, carrying them farther away from the log building. They were in danger of swamping the boat. They did everything they could to stay afloat. Rowing carefully, they managed to keep it steady. But then they remembered something terrible: They'd forgotten to destroy a large gun aboard the ship. Now they saw the pirates getting ready to fire upon them.

From the small boat, Mr. Trelawney tried to shoot the gunner on the ship. His shot missed, but hit another mutineer. The men on the *Hispaniola* continued preparing their big gun.

Trelawney readied himself to fire again. But then the ship's gun went off. The round-shot flew just over the little boat. It hit nobody, but was enough to swamp the boat.

They were near the shore and the water was only three feet deep. But the cargo was at the bottom, and only two of their five guns were saved. They could hear voices in the woods, coming closer to the shore. They had to get to the stockade before the buccaneers saw them. They waded ashore as fast as they could, leaving behind half their powder and food.

As they made their way through the woods, they could hear the footsteps and crackling branches of the buccaneers as they also crossed the woods. The buccaneers didn't know the men were there. Mr. Trelawney and the others had time to get their weapons ready.

Forty paces from the stockade, they came to a clearing. As they stepped toward it, seven mutineers ran into the clearing, too. The pirates were surprised to see Dr. Livesey, Mr. Trelawney and the others. Before they could get their weapons ready, the doctor and two others fired on them. One was killed. The others ran away.

The men reloaded and continued toward the stockade. A gun went off in the woods, and one of Trelawney's men fell dead. The others fired back right away then ran to the stockade. They made it to safety and began to unpack their supplies. From his large pockets, Captain Smollett pulled a folded British flag—the Union Jack. He wasted no time climbing to the roof of the stockade to fly it.

Almost immediately, round-shot flew high over the roof and dropped into the wood. Soon another flew, and fell within the stockade. It scattered sand but did no damage.

"Captain," said Squire Trelawney, "the house is quite invisible from the ship. It must be the flag they are aiming at. Would it not be wiser to take it in?

"Strike my colors?" cried the captain. "No, sir, not I." And, as soon as he had said the words, the others agreed. Not only did the flag make them feel good, it also told their enemies they were not afraid.

All through the evening, the heavy balls kept thundering away, but none did any real damage. The men had ten days' worth of rations. No one knew what had happened to Jim Hawkins. They believed he was probably dead.

He wasted no time jumping to the roof of the stockade to fly it.

Jim Hawkins Continues the Story

I was in the woods with Ben Gunn when we heard the guns on the other side of the island. Soon after, we saw the Union Jack go up.

"Now," said Ben Gunn, "there's your friends, sure enough."

"Far more likely it's the mutineers," I answered.

"Not true!" cried Gunn. "In a place like this, Long John Silver would fly the Jolly Roger—the pirate flag. Make no doubt about that. No. That's your friends. They're probably in the stockade, making the best of it."

"Then I had better get there," said I.

"You go," agreed Gunn, "but I'm going back to my part of the island. I'll meet your friends when the time comes. When Ben Gunn is wanted, you know where to find him, Jim. Just where you found him today. Send the doctor or Squire Trelawney to find me. One or the other. And he's to come alone. I have a matter I need to discuss with him."

"Good," I said, "and now may I go?"

"You won't forget?" asked Gunn, a little nervously. "Then I reckon you can go."

A cannon ball came tearing through the trees and hit the sand close by us. The next moment, each of us had taken to his heels in a different direction.

For an hour, the boom of guns shook the island as the balls came crashing through the woods. I made my way slowly toward the flag. The closer I came, the more danger I was in. As I went, I noticed the white rock in the distance. I wondered if this was the white rock where Ben Gunn said he kept his handmade boat. I didn't have time to check.

I kept moving. Soon enough, I approached the log stockade. I called to whoever might be there. The doctor, squire, captain and the others welcomed me inside.

The captain gave us jobs to do. Some gathered firewood. Others kept watch. When the chance came, I told the doctor about Ben Gunn.

"I'm not very sure whether he's sane," I admitted.

"If there's any doubt about the matter, he is," returned the doctor. "A man who has been three years biting his nails on a desert island, Jim, can't expect to appear as sane as you or me. It doesn't lie in human nature. You said he wanted cheese?"

"Yes, sir, cheese," I answered.

"Well, Jim," says he, "just see the good that comes of being dainty in your food. You've seen my snuffbox, haven't you? And you never saw me take snuff; that is because in my snuffbox I carry a piece of Parmesan cheese—a cheese made in Italy, very nutritious. Well, that's for Ben Gunn!"

Later, the doctor, captain, and squire discussed what to do. Our food would run out long before help came. Our best hope was to kill off the buccaneers until either they surrendered or ran off with the *Hispaniola*. Out of nineteen pirates, four or five were already dead and two others were wounded. They had plenty of rum aboard ship, and, being pirates, would probably drink too much of it. That would help us. In fact, even though we were a half-mile away, we could hear them singing and shouting drunkenly.

I was dead tired and slept like a log of wood. Early the next morning I was awakened by a bustle and the sound of voices.

"Flag of truce!" I heard someone say. Then, with a cry of surprise, "Silver himself!"

Sure enough, there were two men just outside the stockade. One waved a white flag. The other, standing on his crutch, was Long John Silver.

"Keep indoors, men," said the captain to us. "Ten to one this is a trick."

Silver asked permission to come inside the stockade to discuss the truce. The captain gave him permission. Silver went to the stockade wall, threw over his crutch, got aleg up, and lifted himself over the wall and safely to the other side. Then, with some trouble, he worked his way up the hill between the wall and the log shelter we occupied. It was a cold morning, but the captain wouldn't let him inside.

"Well?" said Captain Smollett, as cool as can be.

Silver remarked how clever the captain was for sneaking aboard the *Hispaniola* last night and killing one of the men while the crew lay in a drunken sleep. Captain Smollett certainly had no idea what he was talking about, but pretended that he did. I knew instantly that it must have been Ben Gunn who did this deed. Now we had only fourteen enemies to deal with.

"Why are you here?" asked the captain, lighting his pipe.

"We want that treasure, and we'll have it," said Silver. "That's our point. You have the treasure map, don't you?"

"That may be," replied the captain.

"I know you do," said Silver. "Here's what I propose. Give us the treasure map and we'll give you a choice. After we collect the treasure, you can either come aboard the ship and we'll drop you off someplace safe, or we'll share the treasure with you, but leave you here. When we get back home, we'll send someone to rescue you."

"Is that all?" asked Captain Smollett.

"Every last word, by thunder!" answered Silver. "Refuse that, and all you'll see of me is musket-balls."

"We refuse," replied the captain, calm as can be. "Now get out of here!"

Silver tried to look calm, but had trouble getting up. None of us would help him. With a dreadful oath he stumbled off, fell down in the sand. Trying four or five times, the man with the white flag of truce helped him over the stockade wall. Together they disappeared among the trees.

The captain knew that wasn't the end of the matter. He told us to prepare our guns and keep alert. We were to fire if we saw anyone approach. An hour passed. We strained our ears and eyes for signs of an attack. Suddenly one of our men fired his musket. Return fire rang out all around the log-house. Several struck the walls but none entered.

When all was quiet, we tried to determine how many mutineers were out there, and where they were. We had to protect every side. If they got over the stockade wall, they could shoot us down like rats.

Not much time to think about it. Suddenly, with a loud huzza, a small group of pirates leaped from the woods on the north side and ran straight for the stockade. A musket ball flew in the doorway and knocked the doctor's musket to bits.

The boarders swarmed over the fence like monkeys. We fired again and again. Three pirates fell, but one jumped up again and ran into the woods. Four more pirates came over the wall and raced toward us. None of our shots struck them.

Our position was reversed. A moment earlier we were firing, under cover, at an exposed enemy. Now we were uncovered and could not return fire. The log house was full of smoke from our guns and our fire. Cries and confusion rang in my ears.

The captain called for us to use our cutlasses. The fight continued inside and outside the log house. Somehow we again gained the upper hand. The pirates retreated. In three seconds nothing remained of the attacking party but the five pirates who had fallen.

Back in the log-house we saw that one of our men had been killed, the other stunned by a strike on the head. The captain also had been wounded. We were sad over our losses, but we also had good news. Before, there were seven of us against nineteen of them. Now it was four against eight—much better odds.

A musket ball had broken Captain Smollett's shoulder blade, but he was expected to recover. His leg also had been injured, and the doctor made certain he kept off it.

The mutineers didn't attack again. We ate and began to relax. A little past noon, the doctor picked up his hat, pistols, and his cutlass, put the treasure chart in his pocket and his musket over his shoulder. Then he set out briskly through the trees to meet with Ben Gunn.

The sun beat down on the log house and it grew hot. The dead bodies around me made me disgusted and afraid. Finally, I could stand it no longer. I filled both pockets of my coat with biscuits, picked up two pistols, and snuck out. I knew it was wrong to leave the others, but I was still just a child, and I wanted to find Ben Gunn's boat.

I took the long way around the island to avoid being seen by anyone. The sun was starting to set and the fog was coming in when I saw the white rock an eighth-mile away. Crawling through the brush, it took me a while to reach the boat. I found it under a tent.

It was home-made if ever anything was home-made. The lop-sided framework was made of tough wood covered with goatskin. It was very small, even for me.

I had come to find the boat. Now I had found it. But I wanted to do more. The idea came into my head that the pirates were going to pull up anchor on the *Hispaniola* and sail her away,

The boarders swarmed over the fence like monkeys.

Hands and the other man, who was wearing a red nightcap, were locked together in a deadly wrestle.

leaving us. I intended to stop them with this little boat. My plan was to cut the line, setting the ship to drift aimlessly.

As the last rays of daylight dwindled and disappeared, absolute blackness settled down over Treasure Island. I lifted the boat onto my shoulders and stumbled toward the shore. The pirates' campfire and the lights on the ship helped guide me.

Soon I had reached the water. I put the little boat upon it and climbed in. She turned in every direction except the one I wanted to go in. By good fortune, the tide swept the little craft right toward the *Hispaniola*. I was alongside the ship. I grabbed the line and waited for the right moment to cut it. Each time the ship tilted and the rope slackened, I made a cut. While I waited, I heard drunk, angry voices inside the ship's cabin. One of the voices I recognized as being the coxswain's, Israel Hands. The ship's rope grew slack and I made the final cut. The *Hispaniola* immediately began to sway and spin in the water. The two men on board didn't seem to notice. I knew why when I grabbed the end of the rope and looked in the cabin window. Hands and the other man, who was wearing a red nightcap, were locked together in a deadly wrestle.

I lowered myself back into my little boat, which was riding in the wake of the ship. Suddenly, the *Hispaniola* changed course. It began heading out to sea, taking me and the boat with it! I could do nothing. I lay down in the boat, tossed by the waves and somehow fell asleep.

hen I awoke it was morning. I was still being tossed about in the little boat, on the south-west end of Treasure Island. The jagged rocks and cliffs made it impossible for me to go ashore there. I sat up and tried to steer the boat to a better landing place. I was drenched and terrified, but the boat rode the waves well. I used my cap to bail water out to keep afloat.

Progress was slow. At noon, the sun burned hot and I grew thirsty. I continued moving around the island. Right in front of me, not a half mile away, I saw the *Hispaniola* under sail. I was so thirsty that I didn't know whether to be glad or afraid.

As I watched the ship, I could tell by her motion in the water that nobody was steering. "Clumsy fellows," said I, "they must still be drunk as owls." I decided to try to steer my boat over to the *Hispaniola* and climb aboard. If everyone was still asleep, I could get some water.

It took time, but soon I was close enough to see the decks of the big ship. No sign of anyone. Either the ship was deserted, or the pirates were still below deck. If that were true, I could lock them in and have the ship to myself.

I paddled closer to the ship. My little boat rose up on a swell. Just then, the ship did the same thing—it was moving directly above and was about to crush me! I leaped out of my boat and grabbed the ship's boom. Holding on tight, I swung myself onto the ship, just as my boat was destroyed. I had no way of getting off the *Hispaniola*.

With no one steering, the ship moved with every change of the wind. As I looked around, I found the two men I saw fighting the night before. They were both on the deck. The man with the red cap was dead, probably beaten to death by Israel Hands. I thought Hands was dead as well, but soon he started to moan and move.

When he awakened, I told Mr. Hands that I was now the captain of the ship. I brought him some food and drink, then took down the pirate flag and threw it overboard. I gave Hands a handkerchief to patch up his bleeding leg. Then I began to steer the ship. All the while, Israel Hands watched me with treachery in his eyes.

I needed to bring the ship to the north side of the island so we could land it on the beach. Because I had cut the anchor line, a beach landing was our only hope to stop the ship. I didn't trust Israel Hands, and I kept my eye on him. When the wind died down, he asked me to fetch him some wine from below deck. I thought the request was strange, but I went to get it for him. I went below deck and immediately popped my head out of a different hatch to see what Hands was up to.

He had risen onto his hands and knees. Though his leg was badly hurt, he moved quickly toward a coil of rope on the deck and pulled a knife out of its center. He hid the knife in his jacket and hurried back to where I'd left him. I soon returned with the wine, never letting him know what I had seen.

Israel Hands couldn't steer the ship, so I knew he wouldn't try to kill me until we had landed. In fact, he helped me steer the ship to the beach. The landing was difficult, but together we did it. He issued his commands and I obeyed them until the *Hispaniola* was safely on its way to the wooded shore.

The excitement of steering the ship had made me forget about the danger I was in. As I looked onto the shore, a sound behind me made me turn my head. There was Hands, rushing toward me with a knife in his hand. I dodged out of his way at the last second. Hands, though still hurt, raced after me. I pulled out my pistols and took careful aim. I fired. Nothing happened. The powder was wet and useless. I cursed myself for not reloading earlier.

Hands kept after me, but I managed to dodge him. Then the *Hispaniola* struck ground and tipped at a sharp angle. We tumbled together. I stood up fast and climbed the mast. Hands tried but he couldn't climb after me. That gave me a chance to reload my guns. Then, with a pistol in either hand, I said to him,

"One more step, Mr. Hands, and I'll shoot."

Hands stopped in his tracks. I felt safe now. But he wasn't finished. He pulled out his knife and threw it at me. It scraped my shoulder as it struck the mast. At the same instant, my pistols suddenly fired and tumbled into the sea. They didn't fall alone. Israel Hands, struck by the bullets, fell head first into the water.

Now alone on the ship, I managed to steer it safely ashore. About the same time, the sun began to set. I climbed off the ship and eagerly headed toward the log block-house where I had last seen Dr. Livesey, Squire Trelawney, Captain Smollett and the others. I had to move slowly so the pirates wouldn't find me. The night grew blacker.

At last I got to the block-house. No one was keeping watch and the fire had gone out. In the darkness I was frightened until I heard the calm sound of snoring. I snuck inside to find my own sleeping spot. I thought I would enjoy their surprised faces when they saw me the next morning.

Then, with a pistol in either hand, I said to him, "One more step, Mr. Hands, and I'll shoot."

My foot struck a sleeper's leg. He turned and groaned, but without awakening. And then, all of a sudden, a shrill voice broke forth out of the darkness:

"Pieces of eight! Pieces of eight! Pieces of eight! Pieces of eight!" It wouldn't stop. It was Silver's green parrot, Captain Flint! Then I heard Long John Silver himself cry, "Who goes?"

I tried to run out, but was caught. One of the men lit a torch. I wasn't among my friends—I was in a den of pirates!

In the torchlight I could see six pirates. One was badly wounded. To my surprise, Silver spoke to me as if we were friends. He told me that Dr. Livesey and the rest of my real friends had turned against me because I had deserted them. In a way I was glad to hear this news because it meant they were still alive. He then asked me to join the pirates. I refused.

"You can kill me now," I told him, "or you can spare me. And if you spare me, I can help you later. When we get back home and you and the others are in court for piracy, I'll speak on your behalf. Maybe that will keep you from the gallows."

As Silver thought about my words, some of the other buccaneers sprang at me with knives. Silver stopped them. The pirates were not happy with Silver. They argued and then stepped outside of the block-house to hold a meeting. Silver and I were left inside.

"I want to save you, Jim," whispered Silver, "because I like you, and also because you can save me."

He told me that I was in grave danger from the other pirates. He said he didn't think the pirates would succeed in their mutiny. He admitted that secretly he and I were on the same side. In fact, he had already spoken to Squire Trelawney, who had given him the treasure map! I could not imagine why the squire would part with it.

My life wasn't the only one in danger. If Silver's men suspected that he had turned against them, he'd be in danger too. I peered through a knothole to look for the pirates. About halfway down the slope to the stockade, they were collected in a group. One held a torch. Another, on his knees, held a book and a knife. The others stooped to watch him cut something out of one of the pages. Once they'd finished whatever it was they were doing, they rose and came toward us.

The others stooped to watch him cut something out of one of the pages.

The five pirates entered the block-house. One of them stepped forward and handed Silver something. Silver took it and looked at it—the black spot, cut from a page of a Bible. The pirates were demanding that Long John Silver step down as their leader. They told Silver they were unhappy with him because they should have had the treasure by now. They also thought I should be killed for spoiling their plans to get it.

When it was Silver's chance to talk, he explained that I was still alive because I was their prisoner. Then he showed them the treasure map. The pirates leaped upon it like cats upon a mouse. It went from hand to hand, admired like it was made of gold. The mutineers changed their minds. They wanted to keep Silver as their leader.

That was the end of the night's business. We lay down to sleep. It took a long time before I was able to close my eyes.

Next morning we were awakened by Doctor Livesey. He'd come to the block-house to tend to the wounded pirates.

"Top o' the morning to you, sir!" cried Long John Silver. "We've got quite a surprise for you, too, sir," he continued. "We've a little stranger here. A new lodger, sir."

"Not Jim?" replied the doctor.

"The very same Jim as ever was," said Silver.

The doctor did not seem happy to hear I was safe. He went to work changing the pirates' bandages and giving medicine. When he was finished, he asked to speak with me.

At first, the pirates wouldn't let him. Then Silver allowed it. The doctor had to stand outside of the stockade wall while I stayed locked within. The doctor agreed and started his walk to the wall. When he was on the other side, Silver escorted me to my meeting. We walked slowly; Silver feared the pirates might attack us if they thought we were running off.

When we got to the wall, Silver spoke to the doctor, his voice trembling. He begged the doctor to help save his life, just like Silver had saved mine. Then he left me alone to speak in private with the doctor.

"Jim," he urged, "jump the wall and we'll run for it."

"I can't," I replied, "I gave Silver my word. I trust him with my life." I told the doctor about my adventures. Especially how I had saved the ship and hidden it on the North Inlet. "If something happens to me, get to it before the pirates do," I said.

"At every step you've saved our lives. We'll find a way to save yours, too," the doctor promised.

Silver returned to fetch me back. The doctor told him that if they get off the island, he would do everything he could to save Long John's life. Then he left.

Silver told me we had to stick together if we were to survive. To win the trust of the five pirates, he told them he heard me tell the doctor that the ship was safe. All they had to do was collect the treasure, find the ship, and be gone. Hearing this, I was no longer sure whose side Long John was on. I would have to be very careful.

෴

The time had come to search for the treasure. The buccaneers were in good spirits. I was not. We must have looked ridiculous in our soiled sailor clothes, everyone but me armed to the teeth. Silver had two guns slung around him, besides the great cutlass at his wrist and a pistol in each pocket. To complete his strange appearance, Captain Flint sat perched upon his shoulder, chattering. I had a line around my waist and followed after Silver, who held the loose end of the rope. For all the world I was led like a dancing bear.

The other men carried picks and shovels, food and drink. The party was spread out, up and down the hills. Suddenly, the man farthest in front began to shout in terror. We ran to see what the matter was. He had found a human skeleton. It was an old sailor, and his bones lay arranged like the pointer on a compass. Silver checked his treasure map. Sure enough, the old sailor was pointing the way.

For all the world I was led like a dancing bear.

The pirates determined he was one of Captain Flint's men, killed after helping to bury the treasure. All of us were a little frightened now. We started on. All of a sudden, somewhere out of the trees came the well-known tune and words:

"Fifteen men on the dead man's chest—
Yo-ho-ho, and a bottle of rum!"

The color drained out of the pirates' faces. "It's Flint's ghost!" cried one.

"Wasn't either," said Silver. "That voice had an echo, and ghostly voices don't echo."

The men discussed who or what made the voice. Finally, one of them remembered that Ben Gunn had been marooned here. They figured it was Ben and began to calm down.

"Why, nobody minds Ben Gunn," said one, "dead or alive, nobody minds him."

Our party continued on, following the map. Eventually we neared the end of our hunt. And suddenly, not ten yards away, right where the map said to dig, lay a giant hole. The riches were gone.

Each of the six men acted as if he had been struck. But with Silver the blow passed almost instantly. He kept his head and changed his plan.

The buccaneers leaped into the hole and began to dig with their fingers, looking for any loose coins that might have been left behind. None of them noticed when Silver handed me one of his pistols. They found only one two-guinea piece, which they passed around, grumbling. Then they climbed out of the pit, after our blood. They blamed us for this misfortune.

The five of them stood on one side of the pit. The two of us stood on the other. One of the pirates raised his voice and his arm to lead a charge against us. But just then—crack! crack! crack!—three musket-shots flashed out of the thicket. The pirate tumbled head-first into the pit. Another pirate fell dead, too. The remaining three turned and fled.

Doctor Livesey, Ben Gunn and another from our party came out of the woods.

"Thank ye kindly, doctor," said Silver. "You came in about the nick, I guess, for me and Hawkins. And so it's you, Ben Gunn!" he added. "Well, you're a nice one, to be sure."

"I'm Ben Gunn, I am," replied Ben. "How do, Mr. Silver?"

The doctor and Ben Gunn had saved us, and now we were headed off to Ben's cave, where he had the treasure hidden. On the way, the doctor explained what happened. Two months before we arrived in the *Hispaniola*, Ben had found the treasure and moved it. When Dr. Livesey met with him, he admitted this secret. The doctor knew that the treasure map was useless, and gave it to Long John Silver.

When the doctor learned that I would be with the pirates when they discovered the treasure was missing, he knew they would kill me. He sent Ben Gunn ahead to delay them with his ghostly voices. Meanwhile, the doctor raced to the treasure site with his musket in time to rescue Silver and me. Ben, who could move quickly through the forest, ran to join him.

Soon we arrived at the cave. In the firelight I could see great heaps of coins and stacks built from bars of gold. To be sure, it was a magnificent treasure, but how many lives were lost trying to find and keep it? We ate our dinner and went to bed.

The next morning we awoke early. We had much work to do, moving the great mass of gold nearly a mile to get it aboard the *Hispaniola*. For my part, I was not much use at carrying. I was kept busy all day in the cave, packing the coins into bread-bags. It was a strange collection—coins from all over the world, with pictures of kings and curious designs. I think I never had more pleasure than in sorting them. By evening, a fortune had been stowed aboard the ship, but there was even more to load tomorrow. All this time we heard nothing of the three surviving mutineers.

At last, the ship was loaded and we were ready to sail. We held a vote and decided to leave the three pirates on the island. We couldn't risk another mutiny. We left behind food, medicine, and tools, and sailed away. When last we saw them, they were kneeling together on the shore, begging us to take them with us. It made our hearts sad, but we simply could not.

With so few men on board, sailing was difficult. Everyone had to lend a hand, except for

I think I never had more pleasure than in sorting them.

Captain Smollett, who was still injured. He lay on a mattress and gave his orders. We headed to the nearest port, in Spanish America, to get fresh hands and more supplies. It was just sundown when we cast anchor.

The sight of so many good-humored faces, the taste of the tropical fruits, and, above all, the lights that began to shine in the town, made a most charming contrast to our dark and bloody time on Treasure Island.

The doctor, the squire, and I spent the evening with the captain of an English man-of-war. The day was breaking when we once again boarded the *Hispaniola*.

Ben Gunn was on the deck alone. He told us that Long John Silver was gone, along with one of our sacks of gold coins. I think we were all pleased to be rid of him so cheaply.

Well, to make a long story short, we hired some sailors and made a good cruise home. All of us had ample share of the treasure, and used it wisely or foolishly, according to our natures.

Of Silver we have heard no more. That dreadful seafaring man with one leg had at last gone clean out of my life.

Oxen and wain-ropes would not bring me back to that accursed island. The worst dreams that ever I have are when I hear the surf booming about its coasts, or I start upright in bed, with the sharp voice of Captain Flint still ringing in my ears: "Pieces of eight! Pieces of eight!"